For the children and teachers of Larkrise Primary School, Oxford. T.H.

For Beth, Becky and Caz. S.H.

First published 2018 by Walker Books Ltd, 87 Vauxhall Walk, London SE11 5HJ

2 4 6 8 10 9 7 5 3 1

Text © 2018 Teresa Heapy   Illustrations © 2018 Sue Heap

This book has been typeset in Youbee

Printed in China

British Library Cataloguing in Publication Data:
a catalogue record for this book is available from the British Library

ISBN 978-1-4063-7789-7 (hardback)
ISBN 978-1-4063-8564-9 (paperback)

www.walker.co.uk

6	7	8	9	10
16	17	18	19	20
26	27	28	29	30
36	37	38	39	40
46	47	48	49	50
56	57	58	59	60
66	67	68	69	70
76	77	78	79	80
86	87	88	89	90
96	97	98	99	100

This Walker book
belongs to:

1	2	3	94	5
11	12	13	14	15
21	22	23	24	25
31	32	33	34	35
41	42	43	44	45
51	52	53	54	55
61	62	63	64	65
71	72	73	74	75
81	82	83	84	85
91	92	93	94	95

Ten Cars
and a
Million Stars

A Counting Storybook

Teresa Heapy

illustrated by Sue Heap

WALKER BOOKS
AND SUBSIDIARIES
LONDON · BOSTON · SYDNEY · AUCKLAND

Alice was doing her
best counting for the baby.

"Look, Baby,"
she said.

"Here is **ONE** giant teddy."

"You've got **TWO** floppy bunnies

and **THREE**
shaky rattles ...

and *I've* got **FOUR** smart

penguins, **FIVE** cuddly cats,

SIX friendly monkeys,

SEVEN shy ducks,

EIGHT tiny mice
and NINE big dinosaurs.

Here are **TEN** fast cars, stuck

in a long traffic jam ...

and **TWENTY** silly animals

with **THIRTY** hats

and **FORTY** shoes!

There are **FIFTY** blocks

in our secret den, and ...

this many toys make
ONE HUNDRED!"
The baby was very impressed.

But Alice wasn't finished. "There are bigger numbers than that, Baby. There are thousands of snowflakes in a snowstorm. And millions of stars in the sky!"

Just then Mummy came in.
"We've been doing counting, Mummy,"
said Alice.

"Mummy! Hug!" said the baby.

"Can I have a hug, too?"
asked Alice.

Mummy opened her arms
and she smiled a big smile.
"Not just one," she said.
"More hugs than you can
EVER count!"

1	2	3	4	5
11	12	13	14	15
21	22	23	24	25
31	32	33	34	35
41	42	43	44	45
51	52	53	54	55
61	62	63	64	65
71	72	73	74	75
81	82	83	84	85
91	92	93	94	95

6	7	8	9	10
16	17	18	19	20
26	27	28	29	30
36	37	38	39	40
46	47	48	49	50
56	57	58	59	60
66	67	68	69	70
76	77	78	79	80
86	87	88	89	90
96	97	98	99	100

Also by Sue Heap:

ISBN 978-1-4063-6106-3

Available from all good booksellers

www.walker.co.uk